BOX OF HOPE

Glenna Goodman

dizzyemupublishing.com

DIZZY EMU PUBLISHING

1714 N McCadden Place, Hollywood, Los Angeles 90028

dizzyemupublishing.com

Box of Hope
Glenna Goodman

First published in the United States
in 2022 by Dizzy Emu Publishing

dizzyemupublishing.com

BOX OF HOPE

Glenna Goodman

Box of Hope

By

Glenna Goodman

2021 0801
2022 0128

gpans@aol.com
602-361-0217
June Vision Producation
Rhode Isalnd

                                                    FADE IN:

EXT. STREET - DAY

The streets are quiet. On the ground there lots debris of
papers, posters and newspapers.

Dirt and dust are all over the place. The wind blows the
dirt and paper. One piece of paper blows in the wind, it
moves along the ground till it rests face up as someone
steps on it. The paper has a headline on it "HITLER HAS
INVADED POLAND."

Other newspapers have headlines with about the same subject.
Some headlines read that the ALLIED FORCES ARE LOSING and
POLISH JEWS ARE FORCED INTO GHETTOS.

There are also some about a battle that had taken place over
the past few years.

There newspapers and posters about capturing JEWS and other
war criminals.

The wind keeps blowing paper down the street and the
buildings have shops that have signs are in Hebrew/

All all are deserted.

EXT. ANOTHER STREET - DAY

The street appears clean and busy. People walk up and down
the street. Most of the stores are open, but have a sign
that says NO JEWS ALLOWED.

Posters hung on the windows state WANTED JEWS FOR REWARD and
JOIN THE NAZI PARTY. Everyone walking by the signs and
posters without looking at them.

EXT. UPPER CLASS STREET - DAY

MARY about 45-55 walks down the street. walks up to one
building and goes up the stairs and into the building.

INT, HANNA'S FAMILY APARTMENT - DAY

The apartment looks bright with a huge window in the living
room. Even though appears the place looks big only the
living room with some doors can be seen. HANNA age 25 and
her sister RACHEL age 21, sits on the floor they wrap some

nick knacks and placing them into a box. GOLDIE about 50
joins the room.

                    GOLDIE
          Boys make sure you are careful
          taking those down.

Isaac age 29, Yossil age 27, and CHAIM age 23 are taking
pictures off the walls.

                    ISAAC
          Yes Mama, we are being very
          careful.

Other family members move about helping with the packing.
MOSHE about 52 comes down the hall with boxes.

                    RACHEL
          Papa, I meed some more boxes.

                    MOSHE
          Rachel, please pack as much as you
          can in each box. There is not
          enough space to go around.

                    RACHEL
          Yes, Papa,

Moshe walks over to Goldie. they just look at each other.

                    MOSHE
          This will work Goldie..

                    GOLDIE
          I hope so.

                    MOSHE
          We have to have faith.

                    GOLDIE
          I'm trying.

Goldie starts to cry and Moshe attempts to comfort her.

INT. JOSEF'S APARTMENT BEDROOM - DAY

The apartment lighting makes the room look dark and small.
JOSEF age 28, Only his hands are viable as he goes though
his motions. He lays out a military uniform.

A shirt placed down on top.

A sash placed on top has the NAZI logo.

A Pause.

INT. JOSEF'S APARTMENT - DAY

Follow Josef's feet as he goes from the bedroom into the
living room light is still dark.

A small kitchenette and a set of shelves above it. Very few
things on the shelves, A few pots and pans and a few dishes.
and a small box.

A hand teaches for a light and turns it on. The light
focuses only on the box.

Josef reaches for this box. The light follows the box.

Takes the box from the shelve.

Josef hand opens the box.

A pile of pictures and other things items first on top is a
picture of his PARENTS Josef hands go through the pictures
one at a time. His father is wearing a uniform from the
First World War as a German Soldier, There are other
pictures in the box, and most of them are of his FAMILY,
there is one of when he was very young maybe about five
years old. A picture of his Mother and his siblings when he
was about ten years old and there is no father in the
picture. There is a postcard from New York City that is from
his oldest brother MARCUS is asking him to come to America.
Josef holds this one for a moment.

INT. JOSEF'S APARTMENT BEDROOM - DAY

Josef starts to get dressed.

Still only following his hands. First he puts on his pants.
He puts on his shirt and buttons it. Then puts on the jacket
and there are medals. Josef's hands reach and grab the sash
and slowly pick it up. As he puts it on Josef's face is
revealed in a mirror,

A light comes through the window to brighten up the room.

Josef is not smiling. He takes a deep breath and fakes a
smile.

                    JOSEF
          Well, another day of dealing with
          this stupid war.

He fakes another smile turns and steps away.

INT, HANNA'S FAMILY APARTMENT - DAY

The Once bright room has little light coming through the
closed drapes. The walls are bare. No personal items or
decorations can be seen. The furniture looks bland and
almost out of place.

Boxes have been piled up on one side of the room.

Everyone stands away from the window. There is silence.
Moshe motions to keep quiet and not move.

There is a KNOCK at the door.

Goldie jumps but answers the door, slowly. Mary stands there
with TWO MEN. Goldie gestures for them to come in. Mary
points to the boxes and the two men each pick up a box an
leave.

                    GOLDIE
          Mary, please take care of our
          things.

                    MARY
          As if they were my own.

The two men return and take some more boxes.

                    GOLDIE
          Thank you for doing this.

                    MARY
          Just be safe, I hope to see you
          again when this is all over.

They hug. The men come back for more boxes.

EXT. MILITARY BASE - DAY

A few Military personal come and go outside the base

INT, MILITARY BASE - DAY

Josef stands next to a table, with OSKAR age 28 who has
light blond hair and a strong physical physic. Around them
lots of military personal doing things. Josef sits as he
joins Oskar.

                    OSKAR
          So are you going to let me
          introduce you to this girl i know?

                    JOSEF
          No. I rather you didn't

                    OSKAR
          Why not? She loves military men. I
          would go out with her myself, but I
          have a date with her best friend.
          She has a body on her that....

Josef stops him and listens into another conversation.

                    MAN 1
          Let's go and get some stupid Jews.

                    MAN 2
          I'm ready. Kill all the Jews.

                    MAN 1
          Worthless pieces of crap.

                    MAN 2
          Glad we are on the right side here.
          Lets Go.

These three men walk off as TWO OTHER MEN start fighting

                    OSKAR
          Josef... Are you interested?

                    JOSEF
          Told you, No.

                    OSKAR
          You want to find your own girl?

                    JOSEF
          Well. I think I'll do better. I
          want someone who has a heart. Not
          just a body.

                    OSKAR
          She has a heart. .. and a great
          bod.

This conversation in the background. till Josef pays more
attention to it.

                    MAN 4
          You jerk.

                    MAN 5
          I'm the jerk? you said you did not
          want to go out with her.

                    MAN 4
          I said I wanted to go out with her,
          but after the weekend.

                    MAN 5
          That is not want you said.

                    MAN 4
          Now I can't, you used her.

                    MAN 5
          Well not my fault, you waited.

At that moment Man 5 Hits Man 4. Josef gets up and runs
towards them.

                    JOSEF
          Stop.

                    MAN 5
          Go away.

                    JOSEF
          Do you really want to fight over a
          woman that neither of you are going
          to see again? Do you really want to
          loose your friendship over it?

The two men look at each other. Both pause.

                    OSKAR
          Josef,

The two men stop fighting. Oskar pulls Josef away.

                    MAN 4
          Your right. Sorry. Man I'm sorry we
          should not fight,

                    MAN 5
          Josef's right. Lets just forget
          about it. She is not worth it.

                    MAN 4
          Yeah. Lets just go.

The two men walk away.

                    JOSEF
          Why did ...

                    OSKAR
          You really need to stop doing that.
          You keep stopping fights that you
          have no business being involved in.
          Remember that one from a few years
          back that gave you a scar on your
          arm.

Josef looks at a scar on his arm.

INT. HANNA'S FAMILY APARTMENT VERY EARLY DAY

Hanna and her family do not speak. Dressed in many layers of
clothes and each has a JUDE star on. Each person has one
suitcase.

Moshe Motions to everyone to be quiet as he steps to the
front door. Isaac, Yossil and Chaim follow right behind him.

Moshe cracks the door open.

INT. HALLWAY OF FAMILY APARTMENT - VERY EARLY DAY

Moshe cracks the door slowly and looks around the hall and
tells a few people to go. A few family members quietly go
and Yossil among them.

INT. HANNA'S FAMILY APARTMENT - VERY EARLY DAY

Moshe shuts the door an waits for a few moments. Moshe
points to a few people and still quiet he cracks the door.

INT. HALLWAY OF FAMILY APARTMENT - VERY EARLY DAY

Moshe again looks up and down the hallway. Moshe motions for
a few to go. Rachel, Chaim that are among the few to go.
Moshe quickly and quietly closes the door again.

INT. HANNA'S FAMILY APARTMENT - VERY EARLY DAY

Moshe once again motions for a few people to move near the
door. Goldie and Isaac among them.

Moshe motions to Hanna too.

                    MOSHE
          Hanna come.

Hanna moves closer to the door.

                    MOSHE (CONT)
                 (to Isaac)
          Take care of your mother.

                    ISAAC
          We will Papa.

                    GOLDIE
                 (To Moshe)
          I love you.

                    MOSHE
          I love you too. Be safe my love. I
          will be right behind you.

Moshe kisses Goldie on the cheek. as he slowly cracks the
door.

INT. HALLWAY OF FAMILY APARTMENT - VERY EARLY DAY

Moshe has the door open as Hanna and Isaac step out and
Goldie right behind him. Goldie looks back at Moshe who
motions for her to go.

They slowly and quickly go down the hall.

INT. HANNA'S FAMILY APARTMENT+ - VERY EARLY DAY

A few seconds later Moshe looks around the empty apartment
takes a deep breath with a tear in his eye steps to the door
himself.

INT.. HALLWAY OF FAMILY APARTMENT - VERY EARLY DAY

As Moshe closes the door very quietly, he looks around and
walks down the hall and moves very quietly. He looks strong.

EXT. STREET - DAY

The streets seem quiet and very deserted, no one around.
There are no sounds but that of a HOWLING WIND. Oskar and
Josef take a turn onto the street Oskar hold his gun high,
while Josef holds his gun low.

EXT. STREET - DAY

The two take a turn onto a new street.

                    JOSEF
          So.

                    OSKAR
          So. You changed your mind.

                    JOSEF
          No. You know i want to find a nice
          girl. someone I can really fall in
          love with.

                    OSKAR
          Come on really? Why waste time on
          that now. Being suck with one
          persona day after day.

                    JOSEF
          If you Love someone that much, it
          should be amazing.

                    OSKAR
          You are a dreamer. You always have
          been.

                    JOSEF
          So. I'm a dreamer. If I wasn't then
          I'd have no future.

                    OSKAR
          Well it is good to have me around
          then.

                    JOSEF
          Still don't like my dream about
          going to America?

                    OSKAR
          There is nothing there for me.

Josef pauses for a moment and then follows Oskar one step
behind.

                    JOSEF
          That's what is great about America,
          you can be anything you want. My
          Brother is going to help me. He
          could help you too.

                    OSKAR
          I help you here. I got you into the
          Army here.

                    JOSEF
          So what? What happens after the
          war? I need direction. I can't keep
          following you everywhere.

                    OSKAR
          Like the bar last week.

                    JOSEF
          I hated the bar.

Oskar gives a strange look to Josef.

                    OSKAR
          Seriously? I thought you had fun
          with that girl.

                    JOSEF
          I wasn't with a girl. You were.

                    OSKAR
          Oh that's right.

Oskar smiles.

                    JOSEF
          Why don't you come to America and
          we can find nice girls, get married
          and raise our kids together.

                    OSKAR
          Stop trying to get me to follow
          your dreams.

Josef just looks at Oskar with a frown,

EXT. FRONT OF GOLDBERG BUILDING - DAY

From the Front of the building Josef an Oskar are Slowly
walking. They are on the lookout. They do not see Hanna and
her family all in a single line quietly walking behind the
building.

EXT. BEHIND GOLDBERG BUILDING -DAY CONTINUOUS

Hanna and her family are still in a single line as they walk
carefully and quietly behind the building Isaac and Moshe
are guiding them. Hanna is right behind Moshe.

INT. GOLDBERG BUILDING - DAY CONIFEROUS

There are a few desk, but nothing is on them. The floor is
covered with paper and dirt. The building has a looking of
abandoned for a long time.

Moshe moves some papers from the floor revealing a trap door
that is in the floor.

Each person goes into the trap an closes the door after each
person. Goldie goes through the door. Then Rachel, Yossil.
Isaac. Moshe goes and closes the trap door.

EXT, FRONT OF GOLDBERG BUILDING - DAY

Josef and Oskar are still on the lookout and are walking
towards the building. As they get closer they hear a NOISE.
Oskar Holds his gun up.

                    OSKAR
          Do you hear that?

                    JOSEF
          No.

Oskar points to the building. They walk closer to the
building. Oskar goes full military mode and aims his gun
high as he steps closer, Josef follows, but his gun is down
across his chest aimed down. As they get closer to the front
door. Josef looks up and sees the sign above the door.

"OFFICE of GOLDBERG AND ASSOCIATES", The sign is warm and
the paint is faced and chipped.

INT. GOLDBERG BUILDING - DAY CONTINUOUS

Hanna is about to open the trap door when she hears a Noise
and she looks around to see where the noise is coming from.
Hanna looks at the trap door

Hanna looks up and sees Oskar and Josef and She moves papers
to cover the trap door with her foot.

Josef and Oskar see Hanna who does not move. She is shaking.
she steps back and bumps a desk and papers fall from the
desk and onto the floor and cover the trap door.

Oskar comes closer to Hanna with his gun aimed right at her
face. Josef is behind him.

                    OSKAR
          Where are the others?

                    HANNA
          Other what?

                    OSKAR
          Don't be stupid, the others like
          you.

Oskar shakes his gun in her face.

                    HANNA
          I...I...don't know where anyone is.

                    JOSEF
          Oskar, I think she is alone.

                    OSKAR
          I thought they come in groups. Like
          dogs.

                    HANNA
          I'm alone. Really.

Dakar looks at her and lowers his gun.

                    OSKAR
          Where are the others. Not going to
          ask again.

                    HANNA
          I...said...I...

Hanna is really shaking.

                    JOSEF
          Stop. We know what we need to do.

Oskar plunges forward and pushes Hanna back against the
wall. His left arm lands up across Hanna's throat.

Oskar ignores Josef and has a mean face

Oskar starts to look up and down the front of Hanna.

                    OSKAR
          I have a better option of what to
          do with her.

Oskar tosses his gun to the side and it falls to the ground.

                    JOSEF
          What are you doing?

Oskar with his right hand moves his hands down the front of
her dress. When he reaches the bottom he starts to Lift her
skirt. Oskar starts to kiss her neck.

Josef attempts to pull Oskar of Hanna, but just pushes Josef
to the ground. Hanna is shaking. Josef notices the gun.

Oskar starts to pull up Hanna's skirt.

Josef Picks up the gun and aims it at Oskar's head.

                    JOSEF
          Back off. NOW!

Oskar stops but does not turn around.

                    OSKAR
          Josef really.

                    JOSEF
          BACK UP!

Josef grabs Oskar's Jacket and is able to pull Oskar back.
Hanna is shaking and does not move.

                    OSKAR
          What is wrong with you?

                    JOSEF
          No matter what, you do not have to
          do that.

                    OSKAR
          I can do whatever I want. SHE is
          garbage.

                    JOSEF
          She is not trash.

                    OSKAR
          She is. She is Jewish.

Josef steps back. Oskar steps back too,

                    JOSEF
          We will do the right thing.

                    OSKAR
          With trash, you can do the right
          thing.

Slowly steps back and Oskar steps with him. As they do their
voices get louder and louder as they keep stepping towards
the door.

Hanna does not move and is still shaking. She glances over
to where the trap door is.

IT is covered with paper.

EXT, FRONT OF GOLDBERG BUILDING - DAY

Josef and Oskar are slowly stepping out of the building,

                    JOSEF
          Calm down.

                    OSKAR
          Calm down? we need to take care of
          HER.

                    JOSEF
          I will take care of her.

                    OSKAR
          Want my gun.

                    JOSEF
          I have mine.

Josef looks at his hand and sees two guns. He has Oscar's
gun. He hands it over to Oskar.

                    OSKAR
          Thanks.

                    JOSEF
          Now go back to base and I'll take
          care of the girl and I'll see you
          later.

                    OSKAR
          Remember we are suppose to capture
          and report all Jews.

                    JOSEF
          I know my job.

Josef Looks back at the building. He is not smiling. Then he
looks up above the door to the sign.

                    OSKAR
          Fine I will go.

                    JOSEF
          I'll do the right thing. Trust me.

Oskar runs off in anger.

Josef just stands there then paces back and forth. Looks
around and down at the papers on the ground.

One paper is an advertisement for a church. Another Paper is
a newspaper about a couple celebrating a milestone
anniversary.Then he looks up and notices all the buildings
all have Jewish sounding business names.

Josef paces again. Looks around again. Looks down at the
papers.

His face goes from annoyed to shock to thoughts.

                    JOSEF
          I know what i need to do.

Josef Rushes into the building.

INT. GOLDBERG BUILDING - DAY CONTINUOUS

Hanna has not moved from the spot she is in and shaking.
Josef goes towards her.

                    JOSEF
          Take my hand.

Hanna Looks in the direction of the tunnel door.

                    JOSEF (CON'T)
          Just follow me.

Hanna does not say anything and does what Josef asks by
holding her hand out. Josef grabs it.

Josef slowly moves Towards the door of the building and
looks around. turns to Hanna.

Josef places his gun down next to the door.

                    JOSEF (CON'T)
          Shh!

Josef holding Hanna's hand starts to run.

EXT. FRONT OF GOLDBERG BUILDING - DAY

Josef and Hanna are running though the street. Hanna tries
to keep up with Josef.

EXT. STREET IN FRONT OF CHURCH -DAY

Josef and Hanna come to a street with a church.

Josef stops looks at Hanna. Takes her hand

They run to the the church and up the stairs. Hanna almost
trips on the way up. Josef helps her from falling. When they
get to the top they go in.

INT. CHURCH - DAY

Josef and Hanna run down the aisle still holding hands. An
Altar BOY about age 12 is there putting some things in
place.

                    JOSEF
          Is the priest here?

                    ALTAR BOY
          Yes.

                    JOSEF
          Can you get him for us please. It
          is very important.

                    ALTAR BOY
          Sure. Be right back.

Josef turns and looks at Hanna.

                    JOSEF
          What is your name?

                    HANNA
          My name is Hanna.

                    JOSEF
          Hanna...I'm Josef, Just go along
          with what about to happen. I'll
          explain later.

Hanna shakes her head in agreement.

The PRIEST about 60 walks over to them. Josef is still
holding Hanna's hand.

                    PRIEST
          How can I help you?

                    JOSEF
          My name is Josef and this is Hanna,
          and we want to get married right
          now, with everything going on, we
          don't want to wait any longer.

                    PRIEST
          OK. Then, let's get married.

The Altar Boy walks over and hands the Priest a book.

                    PRIEST (CON"T)
          Thank you.

The Altar boy steps back.

                    PRIEST (CON'T)
          Simple or formal?

                    JOSEF
          Sweet would be nice.

Josef looks at Hanna and smiles.

                    PRIEST
          Sweet it is. We come together to
          witness the marriage of Josef and
          Hanna.

Looks at Josef.

                    PRIEST (CON'T)
          Josef do you take Hanna as your
          lawful wife from this day forward,
          cherish and have and to hold, for
          richer and poorer till death do you
          part?

                    JOSEF
          Yes. Yes I do!

Looks at Hanna.

                    PRIEST
          Do you Hanna take Josef to be your
          lawful husband, from this day
          forward to be loyal, cherish, to
          have and hold,and obey for richer
          or poorer till death do you part?

Both the Priest and Josef look at Hanna.

                    HANNA
          Yes.

Hanna looks at Josef and smiles.

INT. JOSEF'S APARTMENT - DAY

The door opens wide with Josef kicking it open. Josef and
Hanna are standing in the hallway.

                    JOSEF
          Can I carry my bride over the
          threshold?

                    HANNA
          No.

Josef leads the way into the apartment. Hanna looks around
the place.

We see the room as she does. It is dark and basic. One
corner has a kitchen table with a few chairs. Another wall
had a couch and next to it is a table with a radio on it. On
that wall is the only picture in the place, it is a picture
of Josef when he was young with his family. There is bedroom
of to the side and it has the only window in the place. the
other side is a small kitchenette which is where Hanna stops
in front off.

Josef walks to the couch and removes some paper from it.

                    JOSEF
          Can you cook?

                    HANNA
               (in a low voice)
          Yes.

Josef takes the papers and places them on the table. Hanna
watches him move about.

Josef walks over to the Kitchenette right in front of her
smiles at her. He reaches for the box and bumps Hanna as he
teaches it. Josef slowly takes it down and holds it in front
of him for a beat and opens it.

                    JOSEF
          Hanna take of your Yellow star.

Hanna looks at the Yellow star saying JUDE on her coat and
she takes it off and puts it in the box.

                    JOSEF (CON'T)
          Any other Jewish jewelry?

                    HANNA
          Yes.

Hanna looks down and exposes her STAR OF DAVID pendent.

                    JOSEF
          Place it in the box.

Hanna slowly takes off the chain. Gives it a kiss. Places it
in the box.

Josef closes the box and puts the box on the shelve.
Josef sits down. Hanna does not move.

                    HANNA
          Are you going to hurt me now?

                    JOSEF
          No...No...No...I'm not going to
          hurt you at all. You are safe here.

                    HANNA
          What about your friend?

                    JOSEF
          Don't worry about him. He won't be
          an issue, I'm not going to tell him
          anything.

Josef looks at her and around her. Shakes his head.

                    JOSEF (CON'T)
          You need to dress differently.

                    HANNA
          I had some other clothes in a
          suitcase...but it back at the
          building.

                    JOSEF
          I can get that for you. Plus some
          new dresses...Some books,
          magazines, too. You have to look
          the part of a soldiers wife.

Josef motions to the couch.

                    JOSEF (CON'T)
          you can sit down.

                    HANNA
          OK.

Hanna sits down on the couch. Josef grabs a chair they are
facing each other.

                    JOSEF
          Can you make that stuff that is
          made of oats and noodles

                    HANNA
          Kasha?

                    JOSEF
          Yes.

                    HANNA
          Yes of course i can.

Josef gets up and gets some paper and a pencil.

                    JOSEF
          I need to make a list of things to
          get. Dresses, Pants, shirts, Kasha,
          books, magazines, hair and personal
          needs.

Josef continues to add to the list.

INT. JOSEF'S APARTMENT BEDROOM - DAY

Josef comes out of the bathroom in bight cloths.

                    JOSEF
          Oh. You need something to sleep in.

He goes to a dresser an pulls out some Pj's.

                    HANNA
          Thank you.

                    JOSEF
          Bathroom is right in there.

Hanna passes Josef as she goes into the bathroom.

Josef moves to one side of the bed. Just stands there.

Hanna come out of the bathroom.

                    HANNA
          Um.

Hanna looks at the bed.

                    JOSEF
          Don't worry, even though we are
          married. and about to share a bed.
          nothing is going to happen.

Josef gets into bed. Hanna gets into bed. She lays facing
Josef. Josef turns and turns the light off and facing away
from Hanna.

There is no movement or noise.

INT. JOSEF'S APARTMENT - DAY

Josef is dressed in his military uniform, all but the
jacket. Hanna wearing the same clothes as the day before
steps into the kitchen.

                    JOSEF
          Morning. Hope you slept OK.

                    HANNA
          I guess...I did.

                    JOSEF
          I'm about to head out for work. I
          will be late. I have to get the
          things on the list.

Josef is holding the list.

                    HANNA
          OK.

                    JOSEF
          Do I need to add anything?

                    HANNA
          Um...No

                    JOSEF
          OK.

Josef gets his jacket and picks up the sash. Glaces over at
Hanna and puts on his jacket. Hanna does just looks back at
him.

                    HANNA
          Thank you.

                    JOSEF
          Hanna. when I'm not here do not
          answer the phone or the door.

                    HANNA
          OK.

                    JOSEF
          There is a plate on the table for
          you. See you later.

Josef gets to the door. Opens the door. Takes a deep breath
and walks out. fakes a smile. Takes the sash out of his
pocket and puts it on. Hanna locks the door after Josef
leaves.

Hanna goes to the table and sits and examines the plate of
food. She takes a small bite. She smiles. Takes another
bite. she eats the rest of the food.

EXT. STREET - DAY

Oskar and Josef on duty.

A NOISE is heard.

                    OSKAR
          Shh!

They go towards the noise to locate where it is coming from.
A DOG runs out of a trash can and runs in front of them the
trash can falls.

Josef let's out a sign

                    JOSEF
          Glad it was just a dog.

                    OSKAR
          What is with you today?

                    JOSEF
          I got married.

                    OSKAR
          What?

                    JOSEF
          I got married!

                    OSKAR
          Uh. Why?

                    JOSEF
          Well I felt the time was right.

                    OSKAR
          I thought you wanted me to
          introduce to.

                    JOSEF
          ...No. I said no to that.

                    OSKAR
          You are young. have fun, Why get
          married now.

                    JOSEF
          When it feels right. You know.

                    OSKAR
          WHY?

Oskar keeps shaking his head.

                    JOSEF
          She is great. She even shares my
          dream about going to America, you
          can sill join us.

                    OSKAR
          Again with the America thing. NO!
          I'm not going to STUPID America.
          with you and your new wife.

                    JOSEF
          Wow. I just thought we do things
          together throughout our friendship.

                    OSKAR
Not dumb things, like get married
before we are 30. stupid.

                    JOSEF
Stop that. We are friends
regardless if I'm married or
single.

                    OSKAR
Well married people can't date this
hot thing like I been seeing.

                    JOSEF
You can still date.

                    OSKAR
We can't double.

                    JOSEF
Maybe we can. You will like Hanna.

                    OSKAR
If you just date, fine. But you
didn't have to marry. What if she
is bad.

                    JOSEF
Bad? Bad at what?

                    OSKAR
Cooking cleaning Sex.

                    JOSEF
Not worried about that. stuff

                    OSKAR
Why?

                    JOSEF
She makes me happy.

                    OSKAR
Why?...Never mind I Don't want to
hear it.

                    JOSEF
Oskar.

                    OSKAR
Stop...Just Stop.

                    JOSEF
          Oskar, You will see, someday.

                    OSKAR
          Again Stop.

Josef looks at Oskar. starts to say something but stops.

INT, HALLWAY -NIGHT

Josef carrying bags and some boxes stops in front of the
door. Places everything down. Removes his sash and jacket.
places them into one of the bags. Processed to open the
door.

INT. JOSEF'S APARTMENT - NIGHT

Josef comes in carrying bags and boxes and places then down
on the table.

                    JOSEF
          Sorry I'm late, took longer then
          I thought.

Josef starts to go through some of the bags. Pulls some
stuff out and puts them in the icebox.

Josef gets a box and opens it and takes out a dress. and
shows Hanna.

                    JOSEF (CON'T)
          Hope you like it.

Hanna walks over and looks at the dress and smiles.

                    HANNA
          Yeah.

                    JOSEF
          I got some other dresses and
          personal stuff you might need. if I
          missed anything let me know.

                    HANNA
          OK.

Josef continues to pull things out of bags. Including some
Books and magazines.

                    JOSEF
          I thought you might want something
          to read.

Josef places them on the table. Hanna looks at them.

                    HANNA
          Dinner is almost ready. Can you
          clear the table?

Josef moves the stuff from the table to the couch. The boxes
he takes them into the other room.

Dinner is on the table. Josef comes back into the room he
has changed his clothes. Josef sits down and starts to eat.

                    JOSEF
          This is good.

                    HANNA
          Thanks.

They continue to eat.

INT. JOSEF'S APARTMEN - LATER NIGHT

They are done eating atnd Josef clears the table. and starts
to wash the dishes. Hanna looks surprised. She gets up and
helps dry the dishes.

INT. JOSEF'S APARTMENT - DAY

Hanna walks into the kitchen. Josef has already left for
work. Hanna makes some breakfast. Sits at the table where
there are books and magazines. She keeps looking at them.

After cleaning up after breakfast, she goes to the table and
looks at the books and magazines. She moves them and finally
decided to pick one,

Hanna moves to the couch and sits and starts to read it.

There is a KNOCK at the door. Hanna jumps. Another KNOCK.
Hanna jumps again. Another KNOCK. Footsteps of the person
going away from under the door.

INT. JOSEF'S APARTMENT - NIGHT

Josef clears the table as they finish dinner. Hanna drys.

                    JOSEF
          Why were you in that building?

                    HANNA
          What?

                    JOSEF
          Just want to know about you.

                    HANNA
          Josef...I..um...

                    JOSEF
          You are safe here. I will not tell
          anyone.

                    HANNA
          We were escaping to a safe place.

                    JOSEF
          We?

                    HANNA
          Yes. Me and my family.

Dishes are done. Hanna goes and sits on the couch. Josef
takes a chair from the table and sits down facing Hanna.

                    JOSEF
          So they don't know what happened to
          you.

                    HANNA
          They were already in the tunnel.

                    JOSEF
          Tunnel?

                    HANNA
          The tunnel...it was covered by some
          paper...I moved it.

                    JOSEF
          That is why we did not see it.

                    HANNA
          That was the point.

                    JOSEF
          More important that Oskar my friend
          did not see it...Go on.

                    HANNA
          I was last one to into the tunnel
          when you two showed up...I'm...I
          ...I'm worried if they made it to
          the other end. They probably heard
          what was going on with your friend.

Hanna starts to cry.

                    JOSEF
          I think your family made it. Now
          they are worried about you. But you
          are safe. Oskar isn't going to be a
          problem.

                    HANNA
          My family does not know if I'm safe
          or at a camp right now.

                    JOSEF
          You will be reunited with them.
          once this stupid war is over.

                    HANNA
          Stupid?

                    JOSEF
          Yeah stupid. I don't agree with
          what is going on.

                    HANNA
          Oh.

                    JOSEF
          I know I was lost before the war.
          Thought about school Going to
          America. Doing something...What
          were you doing before the war?

                    HANNA
          I was planning on going to college,

                    JOSEF
          And major in what?

                    HANNA
          I wasn't sure. Maybe education, but
          I like art.

                    JOSEF
          Nice. Tell me about your family.

                    HANNA
          I have three Brothers and a sister.
          lot's of aunts, uncles and cousins.
          My oldest brother is married.and
          works in the the family company.
          That is the building you found me
          in. My other older brother is
          engaged. her and her family were
          taken. We don't know where they
          are.

                    JOSEF
          Sounds like you are close to your
          family.

                    HANNA
          Yes we are. Family is everything.
          It's the most important thing a
          person can have. A lesson both my
          parents taught us. Though I'm
          closest to my sister Rachel. What
          about your family.

                    JOSEF
          I don't know my father...he died in
          the first world war. I was about a
          year old. I'm the youngest. All my
          siblings have move to America
          already. My brother Marcus wanted
          me to go before the war, but I
          stayed because of Oskar. He has no
          family. I met him right after my
          family moved from Germany to here.

                    HANNA
          You were born in Germany?

                    JOSEF
          Yes. We moved her to Poland after
          the war to get a fresh start. My
          Mom was always sad, right up to the
          day she died.

                    HANNA
          I am sorry about you loosing your
          parents.

                    JOSEF
          Thank you.

Points to a picture on the wall.

                    JOSEF (CON'T)
          That is the only picture of my
          parents and me I have.

                    HANNA
          Do you have still have plans to go
          to America after the war?

                    JOSEF
          As soon as I can, I'm gone. I even
          got a book about America. Would you
          and your family consider going to
          America after the war?

                    HANNA
          I don't know...I...We...Just want
          to survive.

                    JOSEF
          What does it FEEL like to be
          Jewish?

                    HANNA
          Well before the war, I didn't feel
          any different from anyone else.
          When Hitler came into power, it
          became scary. Even here. When
          Poland got invaded. I...it...Was
          scary and hard to even walk or even
          talk to our non Jewish friends...
          That was sad. When they closed the
          business.That is when my family
          decided to go into hiding. Right
          now I feel that being Jewish is
          like a disease. I was born Jewish.
          It's not like I did anything wrong.
          It's like what your friend said we
          are treated like trash. I hate
          that.

                    JOSEF
          I hate this war. I hate wearing
          that uniform. If I could protect
          every single Jewish person I would.
          and KILL Hitler too.

Hanna looks at Josef strangely.

                    HANNA
          Then why are you?

                    JOSEF
          Well...Oskar got me in.. plus...I
          feel..If I didn't. I would be hurt.

                    HANNA
          Scared of what?

                    JOSEF
          Scared if I didn't join, I would be
          arrested too. It's like you agree
          or you get arrested.

                    HANNA
          Does Oskar agree?

                    JOSEF
          Agree. Not sure...I know he likes
          being part of the army.

                    HANNA
          I'm just scared.

Josef gets up and sits down next to Hanna and puts his arm
around her.

                    JOSEF
          Hitler can't win. Your family will
          be OK. You will be reunited with
          them. 'till then you are safe here.

Hanna cries.

INT. JOSEF'S APARTMENT - DAY

Hanna is reading a book. and she hears a KNOCK at the door.
She jumps. Another KNOCK. A third KNOCK. Hanna does not
move. We HEAR the person step away.

EXT. MILITARY BASE - DAY

Military people are coming in and out.

INT. MILITARY BASE - DAY

Josef and Oskar are in full uniform. Other military personal
around. A group on the other side of the room are laughing.

                    JOSEF
          Where are we on duty today?

                    OSKAR
          I think the same place as
          yesterday.

                    JOSEF
          OK.

                    OSKAR
          Josef...Hello.

Josef is listening into a conversation.

                    MAN 1
          Are you ready?

                    MAN 2
          You know i am.

                    MAN 1
          Then lets get our gear and shoot
          some Jews.

                    MAN 2
              (Laughing)
          Yeah. Some stupid Jews.

                    MAN 1
              (laughing)
          I hate Jews.

                    MAN 2
          Me too.

Josef walks over to them.

                    JOSEF
          What did they do to you?

                    MAN 1
          What do you mean by that?

                    JOSEF
          I mean why do you hate Jewish
          people?

                    MAN 1
          Cause I do.

                    JOSEF
          You need a reason.

                    MAN 2
          No we don't. Jews are stupid people
          and should all die. Just like
          Hitler says.

                    JOSEF
          Stop that. They are good people.

                    MAN 1
          NO they aren't. I'm glad we moved
          them to the ghetto's and to the
          camps.

                    MAN 2
          I agree and that is too good for
          them.

                    JOSEF
                (Raised voice)
          Wrong. They are people. You are the
          one wrong. People are people.

                    MAN 1
          Unless they are Jewish.

                    JOSEF
          Even Jews are people.

                    OSKAR
          Josef!

                    JOSEF
          Jewish people are nice, that my
          wife...My wife...

Josef stops and walks away.

                    MAN 2
          What is his problem.

                    OSKAR
          Don't know, Marriage has changed
          him.

                    MAN 1
          Fix him.

                    OSKAR
          Working on it.

Oskar runs after Josef.

INT. JOSEF'S APARTMENT - NIGHT

Josef and Hanna are sitting and listening to the Radio.

                    RADIO ANNOUNCER
          In the news today. The German army
          advance into Klarlow and recapture
          it.

                    JOSEF
          Hanna.

Hanna starts to cry.

                    RADIO ANNOUNCER
          The Allied troops continue to fight
          the Japanese in the pacific.
          Sevastopol falls to the Falls to
          the Germans. local weather is clear
          today with a high about 65.

Josef sits next to Hanna and gives her a hug.

                    JOSEF
          I believe your family is OK and
          safe. You need to believe that too.

                    RADIO ANNOUNCER
          Now back to the music here is one
          of today's hits.

Hanna puts her head on Josef's shoulder.

EXT. STREET - DAY

Oskar is aiming his gun high.

                    JOSEF
          You don't need to aim all the time.

                    OSKAR
          You never know.

                    JOSEF
          See. My gun is low. I know if i
          need it i can aim it. I don't want
          to accidentally shoot someone.

                    OSKAR
          Marriage has made you soft.

                    JOSEF
          No it has not. I like going home to
          have my dinner made and a clean
          place. Nice to have someone to talk
          to as well.

                    OSKAR
          I don't care about that. I just
          like to have a woman when I want
          one.

                    JOSEF
          Don't you want someone to love.

                    OSKAR
          Love is overrated.

                    JOSEF
          If you ever loved anyone you would
          understand.

                    OSKAR
          I do love...For about an hour at a
          time.

                    JOSEF
          That is not love.

                    OSKAR
          So.. you know what love is.

                    JOSEF
          Yes.

                    OSKAR
          What is it them?

                    JOSEF
          Giving something for someone else
          even if it's risking everything to
          make them happy and safe.

                    OSKAR
          That is crazy.

                    JOSEF
          See you don't know love then.

Oskar stops in his tracks.

                    OSKAR
          You think your wife is so special.

> JOSEF
> To me she is.

> OSKAR
> is she is a good cook.

> JOSEF
> Yes. Actually she is.

> OSKAR
> Then you have to prove it.

> JOSEF
> Huh?

> OSKAR
> I am coming over for dinner and you
> can show me how wonderful your wife
> is and how great of a cook she is.

> JOSEF
> When?

> OSKAR
> Tonight. why wait.

> JOSEF
> Last minute...But...I guess OK. But
> i have to call her first.

> OSKAR
> Fine. lets get back so base and you
> call. her.

They turn around.

INT. MILITARY BASE - DAY

The two walk right past other men who are talking and a few
who are seating in groups. Josef walk right to a phone
booth.

INT. PHONE BOOTH - DAY

> JOSEF
> Dime?...Ah.

He dials the phone.

INT. JOSEF'S APARTMENT - DAY

Hanna sits quietly reading a book. The Phone rings. She
jumps.

INT. PHONE BOOTH - DAY

Josef looks out at Oskar.

                    JOSEF
          Don't answer...Don't answer...

Josef keep reaping.

INT. JOSEF'S APARTMENT - DAY

Hanna Keeps hearing the phone ring. She looks around, but
does not move.

                    JOSEF (V.O)
          Remember do not answer the phone or
          the door.

                    HANNA
          I remember.

Hanna goes back to reading the book.

INT. PHONE BOOTH - DAY

                    JOSEF
          No answer. Good.

Hangs up. Smiles.

INT. MILITARY BASE - DAY

Josef grin fades as he goes to Oskar.

                    JOSEF
          My wife is not answering.

                    OSKAR
          Shopping?

                    JOSEF
          Not sure.

                    OSKAR
          so that means, no dinner?

                    JOSEF
          Not tonight.

Oskar stands secure.

                    OSKAR
          OK...Then. What about tomorrow
          night?

                    JOSEF
          OK...That may work...Will give
          Hanna a day to prepare.

                    OSKAR
          So tomorrow night. But not for just
          me. I want to bring my brother and
          his wife too.

                    JOSEF
          Mm...I...Guess that is OK. so...
          Tomorrow right after work.

                    OSKAR
          Just will need to pick up my
          brother and his wife and I will be
          there.

                    JOSEF
          Good Dinner tomorrow.

Josef looks away.

INT. JOSEF'S APARTMENT - NIGHT

Josef carrying bags as he comes in. He places them on the
table.

                    HANNA
          Josef the table..

                    JOSEF
          Sorry Hanna that I'm late. But I
          have to tell you something.

Hanna turns to him. Nervous.

                    HANNA
          OK.

                    JOSEF
          Oskar, my friend invited himself
          for dinner. At first it was
          supposed to be tonight. I went to
          call you no answer.

Hanna looks at the phone.

                    HANNA
          That was you?

                    JOSEF
          Yes and I'm glad you didn't answer
          the phone.

                    HANNA
          You told me not too.

                    JOSEF
          And you did well for two reasons.
          that and it was supposed to stall
          the dinner.

                    HANNA
          So he is still coming for dinner

Hanna starts to shake.

                    JOSEF
          Yes. Along with his brother and
          wife.

                    HANNA
          So three of them.

                    JOSEF
          YES.

                    HANNA
          We... I...I...can't do this...There
          is no way.

                    JOSEF
          I have a plan.

Josef takes some stuff out of the bag and puts it in the
Icebox.

                    HANNA
          Plan to cover up that I am Jewish..
          or that he might recognizes me.

Josef stands right in front of her.

                    JOSEF
          Let me explain the plan. No one
          will be able to tell.

                    HANNA
          Hope it's a good plan.

                    JOSEF
          Sit and I'll tell you.

Hanna takes some plates and puts them on the table and sits.
Josef sits too.

                    HANNA
          Explain as we eat.

                    JOSEF
          Plan is simple. We are going to
          give you a fake Background.

                    HANNA
          Fake...Like family and background?

                    JOSEF
          Exactly.

                    HANNA
          Still have the same name.

                    JOSEF
          Yes since i already addressed you
          by name. Here are the facts. You
          were born in Lodz Poland and your
          parents are both gone and you have
          no other family that you know of.

                    HANNA
          What about Siblings?

                    JOSEF
          lets just say no...that is to many
          facts for you to remember.

                    HANNA
          OK.

                    JOSEF
          You work at a store and that is
          where we met.

                    HANNA
          How long ago?

                    JOSEF
          About a year ago...Vague is good

                    HANNA
          I should write this down.

                    JOSEF
          No! Writing anything can be found.
          You have to memorize it.

                    HANNA
          OK. Go on.

                    JOSEF
          I thought you were very pretty and
          kept coming into the store and
          finally asked you to have dinner.

                    HANNA
          I happily accepted.

                    JOSEF
          I was very happy about that. And we
          got close pretty fast.

                    HANNA
          The proposal.

                    JOSEF
          Was simple. By the river. I got on
          one knee and asked you to be my
          wife.

                    HANNA
          I accepted.

                    JOSEF
          The wedding was small cause of the
          war and neither of us has family
          around and that is why Oskar did
          not know.

                    HANNA
          Good cover on that.

                    JOSEF
          Let me test you.

                    HANNA
          OK.

                    JOSEF
          So where is your family?

                    HANNA
          I don't have family but Josef.

                    JOSEF
          Do you have an education?

                    HANNA
          No.

                    JOSEF
          You can still say you went to
          school. but no College.

                    HANNA
          I did not go to college. I might
          after the war.

                    JOSEF
          Good. I will test you more. But i
          think you got the idea.

                    HANNA
          Anything that is not traceable no
          details. no proof.

                    JOSEF
          I'll back you.

Josef puts his hand on Hanna's hand but she pulls it away.

INT. JOSEF'S APARTMENT - LATER NIGHT

                    JOSEF
          How did we meet?

                    HANNA
          You kept coming into the store i
          worked...what if he asks what
          store.

                    JOSEF
          The corner store. It;s not in his
          area so he wont know who works
          there.

                    HANNA
          Details...details...

                    JOSEF
          He won't care about that one.

Josef grabs a hand towel from the other side of Hanna
bumping her. Hanna does not react.

                    HANNA
          I think i got it.

                    JOSEF
          I think you do too.

They are laughing.

                    HANNA
          We are hiding that my real past for
          what I need to be.

                    JOSEF
          Just for a few hours.

They continue to do the dishes.

START MONTAGE

INT. JOSEF'S APARTMENT - DAY

Hanna goes though bags.

INT. JOSEF'S APARTMENT - DAY

Places things on the table and grabs a few fruits.

INT. JOSEF'S' APARTMENT - DAY

She opens the Icebox and takes out some meat.

INT. JOSEF'S APARTMENT - DAY

She tenderizes the meat.

INT. JOSEF;S APARTMENT - DAY

She gets a knife and chops some fruit and vegetables,

INT. JOSEF'S APARTMENT - DAY

Hanna stirs some things in a bowl and tastes it. She adds
some salt and stirs some more.

INT. JOSEF'S APARTMENT - DAY

Hanna cleans the room. Picking things up. She lines up books
on the table next to the couch. She sets the table really
nice. Making everything perfect.

INT. JOSEF;S APARTMENT - DAY

Hanna takes off her apron as she goes into the bedroom.

INT. JOSEF'S APARTMENT - DAY

Hanna comes out with a nice dress on. She looks around
smiles.

END MONTAGE.

INT. JOSEF'S APARTMENT - NIGHT

Hanna standing in front of the stove hears the door. She
jumps. Josef opens the door. Oskar is right behind him.
Frank age 30 and LENA age 28 is behind them.

Josef goes up to Hanna and gives her a kiss on the cheek.

                    JOSEF
          Hanna, this is my friend Oskar and
          this is his brother Frank and his
          wife Lena.

                    HANNA
          Hello, dinner will be ready soon.

                    OSKAR
          Hello Hanna.

                    FRANK
          Hi.

                    LENA
          Hi.

                    OSKAR
          It's been a day. Can we sit down.

                    JOSEF
          Sure.

Josef shows them the table and they sit down. Hanna Gets a
plate of appetizers and puts that on the table and sits down
too.

                    LENA
          So Hanna. how did you and Josef
          meet.

                    HANNA
          At the store I was working at.

Hanna looks at Josef and smiles.

                    JOSEF
          I kept going in, took me a while to
          get my courage to ask her for
          dinner.

                    HANNA
          He was cute about it too. Glad he
          finally asked.

                    FRANK
          Did you guys here about the troops
          in England?

                    OSKAR
          Yeah. I think..

                    JOSEF
          Anyway...I think that America is a
          good place to go. Frank do you
          think that Oskar should go with
          Hanna and I after the war?

                    FRANK
          I think that it's His choice.

                    LENA
               (TO Hanna)
          Are you going to have kids soon?

                    HANNA
          Maybe after the war and when we are
          settled in America.

Hanna gets up and gets some plates from the counter and
places them on the table.

                    OSKAR
          What is that.

Hanna just realized that one of the dishes she made has a
Jewish flavor to it.

                    HANNA
          Um.

                    JOSEF
          Is this one of the recipes that you
          made from one of the cookbooks I
          bought for you?

                    HANNA
          Yes.

She exhales.

                    LENA
          So...Tell us about your family.

                    HANNA
          I don't have family...But Josef.

                    LENA
          What happened to your family.

                    HANNA
          Died when I was young.

                    LENA
          Oskar lost everyone but Frank when
          he was young too.

                    HANNA
          Do you have kids yet?

                    LENA
          We have one son...We plan on having
          more after the war.

                    JOSEF
          Be nice is Oskar could settle down
          and have kids too.

                    FRANK
          Your funny. Josef. Oskar is not the
          settle down type.

                    OSKAR
          I like woman, and I will not allow
          anyone to tie me down.

                    JOSEF
          Been the best think I ever did is
          marry Hanna.

Josef looks at Hanna and has a huge smile. Hanna smiles
back.

                    OSKAR
          I don't need to get married. I have
          everything I need from women.

                    JOSEF
          No you don't you do not have
          someone to share things with and
          have a future with.

                    OSKAR
          I don't need that.

                    LENA
          I remember that feeling when Frank
          and I first got married.

                    HANNA
          How long have you two been married?

                    LENA
          Five years.

                    HANNA
          Still happy?

                    LENA
          You can say that.

Lena looks at Frank and no smile. Frank does not even look
at her. Hanna and Josef look at each other and smile.

                    OSKAR
          Still do not know why you got
          married.

                    JOSEF
          Sometimes you just have to follow
          your heart...not what others say or
          do.

                    HANNA
          So true.

They smile at least other with huge grins.

                    OSKAR
          I'm not getting married

                    JOSEF
          Seems you never will. But i can
          say.You are missing out.

INT. JOSEF'S APARTMENT - LATER NIGHT

Hanna is clearing the last of the dishes from the table.

                    FRANK
          Thank you for having us for dinner.

                    LENA
          It was very good. You are a good
          cook. Josef is lucky to have
          someone who cooks that cook.

                    HANNA
          Thank you.

                    LENA
          And I would like that recipe.

                    HANNA
          I'll write it down for you.

                    LENA
          Thanks.

                    OSKAR
          OK. Enough. I'm tired. and still
          need to work tomorrow.

                    JOSEF
          OK see you tomorrow.

                    FRANK
          We are going Thank again for
          dinner. Good night.

                    HANNA
          Good night and you are welcome.

                    LENA
          Good night.

                    OSKAR
          Night.

They leave. Josef takes a deep breath as he closes the door.

                    JOSEF
          Wow.

                    HANNA
          Sorry I didn't mean to make that
          dish.

                    JOSEF
          I know it's OK.

                    HANNA
          Thanks for covering.

                    JOSEF
          it's OK. don't worry.

                    HANNA
          How do you think things went
          otherwise?

                    JOSEF
          It went OK. Oskar still a jerk.

                    HANNA
          Frank and Lena seem nice though.

                    JOSEF
          Seems Frank got the nice in the
          family.

They both laugh. Hanna starts to clean up. Josef goes to the
couch and picks up the paper and reads.

INT. MILITARY BASE - DAY

Josef Arrives for duty. Oskar is already there. Oskar Loads
two guns and gives one to Josef.

                    OSKAR
          Ready?

                    JOSEF
          Sure.

Josef takes one gun and they walk out.

EXT STREET - DAY

Oskar and Josef are on duty. Oskar is aiming his gun ready.
Josef has his to his side

                    JOSEF
          You enjoyed dinner last night?

                    OSKAR
          Yeah.

                    JOSEF
          My wife is amazing isn't she?

                    OSKAR
          She's pretty. But you did not have
          to get married to have that.

                    JOSEF
          Why are you so against me being
          married?

                    OSKAR
          Cause marriage is stupid.

                    JOSEF
          Why?

Oskar stops and puts his gun down.

                    OSKAR
          Why get married if you just be with
          someone and not have to buy her
          things.

                    JOSEF
          Is this about money?

                    OSKAR
          Josef...This is about money,
          feelings. caring. who needs all
          that?

                    JOSEF
          I do.

                    OSKAR
          Well you are crazy.

                    JOSEF
          I'm not crazy. Hanna is amazing and
          I'm lucky to have her in my life.

                    OSKAR
          You're an idiot.

                    JOSEF
          Well she IS a good cook.

                    OSKAR
          It was good. Still trying to figure
          out what that was. I never seen it
          before.

                    JOSEF
          She found it in a cookbook that I
          gave her.

                    OSKAR
          Well, I can say this. It was not a
          polish dish.

                    JOSEF
          I know that.

                    OSKAR
          Was it German?

                    JOSEF
          No. It was just a dish. Could be
          American.

                    OSKAR
          Do NOT start with that crap too.

                    JOSEF
          What?

                    OSKAR
            (Sarcastic)
          You keep mentioning that you want
          to go to America and have this
          wonderful life. You even want me to
          go...No thank you. STOP it.

                    JOSEF
          Well, I thought we are friends.

                    OSKAR
          You are Not asking like we are.

                    JOSEF
          I changed.

                    OSKAR
          Obviously.

Oskar turns and aims his gun high.

                    JOSEF
          I wanted to share with you.

                    OSKAR
          You can stop.

                    JOSEF
          No. You still did not give me a
          reason not to go to America. You
          have nothing here.

                    OSKAR
          I have my job here.

                    JOSEF
          What job? The military? You know
          the war will end at some point.

                    OSKAR
          I can still be military after. Rise
          in ranks.

                    JOSEF
          With that attitude?

Oskar stops in his tracks again.

                    OSKAR
          Nothing wrong with my attitude. I'm
          doing just fine. Remember I was the
          one who got you in. You want out
          you go and leave me alone.

                    JOSEF
          No wonder you don't want to get
          married. No one wants too.

                    OSKAR
          Now you are just being mean.

                    JOSEF
          You been mean to me ever since I
          told you I got married.

                    OSKAR
          Maybe cause I wanted to double date
          with this girl and her very hot
          sister, who I was to date. When you
                    (MORE)

                    OSKAR (cont'd)
got married she would no go out
with me with out her sister having
a date too.

                    JOSEF
Don't you have other friends then
me?

                    OSKAR
No.

                    JOSEF
What does that say about you?

                    OSKAR
That I valued our friendship.

                    JOSEF
I can still be your friend and be
married. If you are married too, We
can all be friends.

                    OSKAR
Yeah like my brother and his wife?

                    JOSEF
They seem nice.

                    OSKAR
They fought all the way home.

                    JOSEF
Why?

                    OSKAR
Cause you and Hanna were being so
cute giving loving e looks and
sharing dreams.

                    JOSEF
Well maybe in ten years Hanna and I
will be different with kids and
work we will be tired and just glad
to get out of the house too.

                    OSKAR
Does not matter, cause Lena kept
asking me when I was getting
married.

                    JOSEF
          Well tell her when you meet a nice
          girl you will.

                    OSKAR
          Why? I don't want to get married.

                    JOSEF
          It'll get them off your back.

                    OSKAR
          Oh.

                    JOSEF
          See I'm still your friend.

Oskar looks at Josef and smiles.

INT. JOSEF'S APARTMENT - DAY

Hanna is sitting on the couch and reading a book. There is
KNOCK at the door. Hanna Jumps. She looks around does not
move. Another KNOCK. Hanna closes the book and quietly
stands up shaking. She looks around the room. Another KNOCK.
Hanna makes a quiet and quick run into the bedroom

INT. JOSEF'S APARTMENT BEDROOM - DAY

Hanna runs into the room and looks around quickly and runs
into the corner and covers herself up.She is still shaking.

INT. JOSEF'S APARTMENT - DAY

The person knocking walks away.

INT. JOSEF'S APARTMENT BEDROOM - DAY

Hanna is shaking and does not move.

INT. JOSEF'S APARTMENT - NIGHT

Josef comes home and takes off his sash and jacket right
away. He looks around the room. Table is not set. No dinner
is cooking. The book on the couch. silence.

                    JOSEF
          HANNA!

He looks around more.

                    JOSEF (CON'T)
          HANNA!

He opens some doors but no sight.

                    JOSEF (CON'T)
            HANNA

Still no reply. He puts his hand over his mouth and starts
to tear up. He walks into the bedroom.

INT. JOSEF'S APARTMENT BEDROOM - NIGHT

Josef walks into the bedroom. He has tears in his eyes. He
looks around.

                    JOSEF
          HANNA!

Josef looks around. He opens the closet Nothing.

He looks at the floor seeing something shaking. He goes over
to it. He takes the blanket off and reveals a shaking Hanna.

                    JOSEF (CON'T)
          Hanna. Oh my. Are you OK?

                    HANNA
          There...there...

Points to the door.

                    JOSEF
          There?

                    HANNA
          Someone...knocked on the door
          and and...and...I was afraid that
          they found me out and...ready to
          take me away.

                    JOSEF
          I talked to Oskar and he didn't
          know what type of food it was. I
          told him it was American. He
          accepted that.

                    HANNA
          Really?

                    JOSEF
          Really!

                    HANNA
          So they still don't know?

                    JOSEF
          To them you are just a polish girl
          married to a solider.

Hanna takes a breath and stops shaking. Josef gently wipes a
tear from her eye.

                    HANNA
          So I'm safe?

                    JOSEF
          Yes you are safe.

Hanna Jumps up and jumps into Josef arms.

START MONTAGE

EXT STREET - DAY

Josef is on duty with Oskar leading the way. Josef follows a
few steps back.

INT. JOSEF'S APARTMENT - DAY

Hanna places a new table cloth on the kitchen table. She
looks back at it. Pauses for a second and places a plant at
the center. Steps back. Re centers the plant.

INT. EXT. STREET / BUILDINGS - DAY

Josef and Oskar are on duty going in and out of buildings.
They look around and find nothing. They go into several
buildings and still find nothing.

INT. JOSEF'S APARTMENT - DAY

Hanna is cooking a meal. Tasting it and adding things.
Tastes it again. stirs.

INT. MILITARY BASE - DAY

Josef and Oskar having lunch.

> OSKAR
> Still can't believe you got
> married.

> JOSEF
> Still can't believe you are still
> angry at that.

> OSKAR
> Not angry.

> JOSEF
> Sounds it.

> OSKAR
> Mot made.

> JOSEF
> Then what is it.

> OSKAR
> Don't know.

Josef gets up and collects his tray.

> JOSEF
> whatever it is. I'm happy.

He walks away

INT. JOSEF'S APARTMENT - DAY

Hanna is reading a book and listening to MUSIC on the radio.

EXT. STREET - DAY

Josef is caring bags from a store.

INT. JOSEF'S APARTMENT - NIGHT

Josef and Hanna play a board game.

INT. JOSEF'S APARTMENT - DAY

Calendar on the wall changes and the date now reveals it is
May 1945

EXT. STREET - DAY

Josef is caring bags from a store.

END MONTAGE

INT. JOSEF'S APARTMENT - NIGHT

Hanna cooking dinner. Her hair is down and very different
from before. Josef comes home.

                    JOSEF
          Sorry I'm late.

                    HANNA
          Was Oskar giving you a hard time
          again?

                    JOSEF
          Yeah he...

Josef stops as he looks at Hanna.

                    JOSEF (CON'T)
          Your hair?

                    HANNA
               (touching her hair)
          Do you like it?

                    JOSEF
          Yes. Yes I do.

He walks over to Hanna and gives her a hug. Hanna accepts
the hug.

                    HANNA
          Dinner will be ready in a few
          minutes

                    JOSEF
          OK. I just need to take off this
          stupid uniform.

He walks into the bedroom.

                    HANNA
          You know you should not let Oskar
          effect you that way.

Comes out of the Bedroom wearing different cloths.

                    JOSEF
          I never used to let it bother me.
          Now everything he says bothers me.

                    HANNA
          I think you have changed.

                    JOSEF
          Changed?? No. Just realized that
          I do not agree with him. He and I
          used to be friends. But in the past
          few years... since the war...maybe
          before the war...He changed. He
          treats people like dirt.

                    HANNA
          Treats you like dirt too.

                    JOSEF
          Dirt or just wants me to agree with
          him. I just can't do that anymore.

Hanna takes some dishes and places them on the table.

                    HANNA
          Hope you like this...I tried a new
          recipe.

                    JOSEF
          Jewish food?

                    HANNA
          No. American.

                    JOSEF
          Nice.

Josef sits down. Hanna sits down too.

                    HANNA
          I saw it in one of the magazines
          you gave me. I know you want to go
          to America so I thought I would try
          it.

Josef looks it over. Takes a small bite. Then takes a huge
bite.

                    JOSEF
          This is very good.

                    HANNA
          Thank you.

                    JOSEF
          Thank you for thinking about my
          future...But...what about your
          future. What are you doing to do
          after all this?

                    HANNA
          Um... I really do not know...I
          guess I just need to find my family
          and then figure things out from
          there.

                    JOSEF
          Have you or your family ever
          thought about going to America?

                    HANNA
          We never talked about it. I think
          we were just to busy trying to deal
          with everything going on now, to
          even think about the future.

                    JOSEF
          Well...Now you can...I mean for
          yourself. Do you want to go to
          America?

                    HANNA
          Since you talk about it so nicely,
          Maybe...it is a thought.

                    JOSEF
          You can do whatever you want.

                    HANNA
          I never really had that choice
          before.

                    JOSEF
          So much bad stuff is going on. I
          been hearing about battles and how
          the Germans are treating people.
          I'm so ashamed of it all.

He puts his fork down. and starts to cry. He turns his head
so Hanna really can't see.

                    HANNA
          It's OK.

She places her hand on his shoulder and he places his hand
on her hand.

                    JOSEF
          I'm OK. Thanks.

Josef composes himself and continues to eat.

                    HANNA
          Glad you like like it.

                    JOSEF
          It's been a while, but on Friday
          can you make a shabbos dinner?

                    HANNA
          Of course, I just need a few
          things.

                    JOSEF
          Just make a list and I'll get you
          anything you need.

Hanna gets up and gets some paper and a pencil.

INT. MILITARY BASE - DAY

Oskar and Josef are just coming back from duty. Josef takes
off the sash.

                    OSKAR
          You are not supposed to take that
          off.

                    JOSEF
          Don't care.

                    OSKAR
          Anyway. A few of us guys are going
          over to the corner bar. Do you want
          to come with us?

                    JOSEF
          No.

                    OSKAR
          Why not?

                    JOSEF
          I want to get home to Hanna.

                    OSKAR
          Come on! She does not tell you want
          to do. If you want to hang out with
          the boys, I think you are allowed
          too.

                    JOSEF
          It's not that. Hanna has a special
          dinner waiting for us tonight.

Oskar rolls his eyes.

                    OSKAR
          See getting married was stupid. Now
          you can not even hang with friends.

                    JOSEF
          I can. But not tonight.

                    OSKAR
          She's got you by the balls.

                    JOSEF
          Better her then you.

Oskar crosses his arms.

                    OSKAR
          Come on man.

                    JOSEF
          You are a jerk. Do you know that?

Josef walks away.

                    OSKAR
          No I'm not. I am trying to be your
          friend.

                    JOSEF
          Friends support each other. You
          don't I have to go now.

Josef is out of sight.

EXT. GOLDBERG BUILDING - DAY

Josef is walking to the building.

INT. GOLDBERG BUILDING - DAY

Josef walks in and looks around.

                    JOSEF
          Now where it is?

He looks around. more. Picking things up.

                    JOSEF (CON'T)
          I know it is here somewhere.

Keeps going through things.

                    JOSEF (CON'T)
          Come on!

Out of the corner he sees it. Josef walks to the wall and
moves paper and other thing and reveals a blue suitcase.

He picks it up, removes dirt and dust from it. It is still
locked. Slowly goes to the door, looks around. and run out.

INT. JOSEF'S APARTMENT - NIGHT

Josef is carrying the suitcase as he comes home. Hanna sees
the suitcase immediately

                    HANNA
          Josef! My bag! I thought I wold
          never see that again.

                    JOSEF
          I thought you might need it as some
          point.

                    HANNA
          Like if I go to America? or find
          my family?

                    JOSEF
          Yes.

Hanna runs over to Josef and gives him a hug.

                    HANNA
          This is very thoughtful of you. It
          means a lot. Thank you. Thank you.
          Thank you.

                    JOSEF
          You are very welcome.

                    HANNA
          But how?

                    JOSEF
          I just went to the building and
          found it. I thought it was
          important that you have it.

                    HANNA
          Again thank you. Thank you. Thank
          you.

Hanna takes the bag and goes into the bedroom.

INT. JOSEF'S APARTMENT - NIGHT

They just finished dinner and Hanna is washing the dishes.

                    JOSEF
          Do you mind if I listen to the
          radio?

                    HANNA
          You never have to ask. This is your
          home.

                    JOSEF
          Oh.

Josef turns the radio on and a song is playing.

                    JOSEF (CON'T)
          Hate this song.

He changes the station.

                    JOSEF (CON'T)
          I like this song. Do you like it?

Hanna pauses for a moment to listen.

                    HANNA
          It's got a good beat...Yeah...I
          like it.

                    JOSEF
          Why don't you come and sit and
          listen with me.

                    HANNA
          Just about done with the dishes.

Hanna finishes with the dishes and joins Josef on the couch.

                    JOSEF
          You know this is your home too?

                    HANNA
          Oh.

A new song plays.

                    JOSEF
          OH. I love this song.

Josef stands up, dances for a second. looks at Hanna and
stops.

                    HANNA
          You look funny.

Hanna starts to laugh.

                    JOSEF
          I think this is the first time I
          ever saw you laugh...I like it.

                    HANNA
          Have not had much to laugh about.

                    JOSEF
          You will again...soon.

He kneels in front of her.

                    RADIO ANNOUNCER
          Sorry to interrupt the great music
          we are playing. but we have a News
          bulletin we must announce.

Josef leans in to turn the volume up.

                    RADIO ANNOUNCER (CON"T)
          The latest on the war. The Allied
          forces are making advances in the
          Atlantic. The Battle in Okinawa
          Japan and Luzon still are going
          strong as well as Battles in the
          Phillippnes.

Hanna puts her hands on her face. Josef sits next to her and puts his arms around her.

                    RADIO ANNOUNCER (CON'T)
          On local news, after the death of
          Adolph Hitler and his successor who
          has recently taking over is Navy
          Officer Karl Donitz. The battle of
          Berlin is lost and the German army
          has surrendered to Russians.
          Repeating the German army has
          surrendered to the Russians after
          the loss in the Battle of Berlin.
          The war in Germany is over. More
          will follow as more details come
          available.

Josef stands up and starts to dance.

                    JOSEF
          The war is over...the war is
          over... the war is over...

Grabs Hanna and they dance together.

                    RADIO ANNOUNCER
          Now back to our regular scheduled
          programming.

Hanna stops dancing.

                    JOSEF
          The war is over... Why are you not
          happy?

                    HANNA
          What does it all mean?

                    JOSEF
          Means that Hitler lost. You are
          safe. We...you won. the good guys
          won.

Josef walks over to Hanna and puts his hands on her shoulders. She moves and starts to cry.

                    HANNA
          My family.

                    JOSEF
          They are probably safe and now you
          can be reunited with them. Maybe go
          to America...or where ever you
          want.

                        HANNA
              I...I...I'm safe?

                        JOSEF
              Yes. You survived. You are alive
              and well. I kept you alive through
              this stupid war.

                        HANNA
              I am safe.

Hanna starts to dance. Josef joins. After a few moments
Josef stops dancing.

                        JOSEF
              You are safe.

                        HANNA
              I am Safe

                        JOSEF
              YOU ARE SAFE!

                        HANNA
              I AM SAFE!!

Hanna is screaming and happy.

                        JOSEF
              Stop.

                        HANNA
              What is the matter?

                        JOSEF
              I was...I'm still a apart of the
              German Army.

                        HANNA
              Yes I know.

                        JOSEF
              But I was part of it.

                        HANNA
              And hated every second of it.

                        JOSEF
              Enough to hide a Jewish woman right
              in their faces.

                    HANNA
          What do you mean?

                    JOSEF
          You know I was protecting you not
          just from Oskar, but from the
          Germans too.

                    HANNA
          Yes.

                    JOSEF
          So. Now I have to pay the price.

                    JOSEF
          The price for what?

                    JOSEF
          For my part.

                    HANNA
          Protecting me?

                    JOSEF
          I have no regrets for that.

                    HANNA
          Then price for what?

                    JOSEF
          For being a German solider.

                    HANNA
          Maybe they will not have too.

                    JOSEF
          Maybe. But...

Josef goes to the kitchen.

                    HANNA
          Maybe they will take consideration
          what you did for me.

                    JOSEF
          Maybe.

Josef reaches and gets the box.

                    HANNA
          Josef.

                    JOSEF
          I want you go to go find your
          family. I hope they all survived.
          Then go to America.

Josef holds the box in front of him.

                    HANNA
          I need to...?

                    JOSEF
          Do not forget this.

He opens the box. Looks at the items in the box. Including
Hanna's Jewish Pendent star, the Jude yellow star and
Postcards and pics.

                    HANNA
          Oh...That is where that is. I
          forgot.

Hanna moves and stands in front of Josef. He takes out
Hanna's Jewish star. Kisses it and takes Hanna's hand it
places the chain into her hand.

Hanna looks at it. Takes it. Looks at it. Takes the pendent
Kisses it and then puts the chain around her neck.

                    JOSEF
          That is where it belongs. Looks
          good on you.

Hanna starts to tear up.

                    HANNA
          Thank you for protecting me for all
          this time.

                    JOSEF
          I am honored.

                    HANNA
          See, nothing bad hold happen to
          you.

                    JOSEF
          Regardless of what happens to me. I
          want you to have a life. Tell me
          that you will try to get your
          family to go to American and have a
          life.

                    HANNA
          I will talk to them, once I find
          them. That is all can say for now.

                    JOSEF
          That works for me.

Josef goes to hug Hanna. She hesitates for a second then
allows him too. She hugs him back. Both are teary.

Hanna breaks the embrace and looks for some things in the
kitchen.

                    JOSEF (CON'T)
          What are you doing?

                    HANNA
          I think if you are going to be in
          trouble, you will need a good meal
          first. What would you like.

                    JOSEF
          We already had dinner.

Hanna looks at him and sighs. Josef walks over to her and
puts his hand on hers.

                    HANNA
          Well tomorrow you need a good meal.
          I will make a list of things I
          need.

                    JOSEF
          I can't go out....But you can. I'm
          a war criminal. But you are safe
          now.

Josef walks to the other side of the room.

                    JOSEF (CON'T)
          I'm going to miss you.

Hanna turns and looks at him.

                    HANNA
          Josef...I...I ...I'm happy that you
          married me...Even if it was just to
          save my life.

Hanna turns around faces the wall.

                    JOSEF
          Hanna

Hanna turns and faces Josef. Josef looks at her right in the
eye. He walks over to her. Pauses. Then leans in and kisses
her gentle on the mouth.

Silence

Hanna turns and starts to clean the kitchen.

INT. JOSEF'S APARTMENT - DAY

Josef and Hanna are listening to the radio. Hanna is playing
with her chain.

There is a strong pounding knock on the door.

                    OSKAR (V.O.)
          Josef!!

Josef answers the door. Oskar runs in.

                    JOSEF
          Oskar.

                    OSKAR
          Hide me.

                    JOSEF
          What?

                    OSKAR
          Protect me?

                    JOSEF
          From what?

Oskar keeps looking around the place.

                    OSKAR
          They are not here are they?

                    JOSEF
          Who?

                    OSKAR
          The Allied force Police.

                    JOSEF
          No. Why are you asking?

                    OSKAR
          I went out and when I got home they
          were knocking on my door. They have
          come to arrest me. They are coming
          for you too.

He looks at Josef.

                    OSKAR (CONT)
          How are you so calm.

                    JOSEF
          Not worried about being arrested.
          whatever happens happens.

Josef looks at Hanna

                    OSKAR
          Really?

                    JOSEF
          Yeah really. No one has me here
          yet. So I'm going to enjoy whatever
          time I have with Hanna.

                    OSKAR
          If you were single, We could go and
          run and hide.

                    JOSEF
          I'm not hiding.

                    OSKAR
          Can you hide me?

                    JOSEF
          No.

                    OSKAR
          What kind of friend are you?

                    JOSEF
          I guess a bad one.

                    OSKAR
          HIDE ME. HIDE ME!

Oskar starts to cry.

                    OSKAR (CON'T)
          Hide me!

                    JOSEF
               (Sternly)
          No!

                    OSKAR
          After a lifetime of friendship, you
          wont help me now. I always helps
          you.

Josef looks at Hanna. Looks at Oskar. Looks at the picture
of his family on the wall. looks at Oskar again.

                    JOSEF
          Friends. We might have been friends
          at first. But over the years you
          have become irritating and
          annoying. I hate the way you treat
          woman. I hate that you degree me. I
          have done whatever you wanted, even
          if I didn't agree cause I was your
          friend. But over the years
          especially int he last few years I
          have not agreed with anything you
          have done or said about ...about
          just about everything. When we
          first met I was lost. I'm not lost
          anymore...and speaking of the war.
          I hate the war. I don't agree with
          what it stands for. Hitler is a
          psychopathic looser and I'm glad he
          is dead and the Germans lost...

Josef looks at Hanna. Hanna nods her head. Josef looks at
Oskar and points to Hanna.

                    JOSEF (CON'T)
          Do you recognize her? Do you?

Oskar looks at Hanna. shakes his head no.

                    OSKAR
          Should I?

                    JOSEF
          Look at her. Does she look
          familiar?

                    OSKAR
          No!

                    JOSEF
          Years back. In an abandoned
          building in the Ghetto There was a
          woman there. do you remember that?

                    OSKAR
          I...I... I think so.

                    JOSEF
          You were going to rape her and
          arrest her. Do you remember that?

                    OSKAR
          Oh. Yeah I do.

                    JOSEF
          This is her. Hanna is that woman. I
          married her. to protect her from
          You and all the rest of the Nazi's.

                    OSKAR
          YOU HID HER!

Josef pushes him down to the floor

                    OSKAR (CON'T)
          You are a traitor...If I knew I
          would have turned her in...You too.

                    JOSEF
          That is why I didn't tell you. oh
          that dish you did not know. it was
          a Jewish dish.

There is a KNOCK on the door. Josef drops Oskar to the
floor.

Oskar gets up and runs into the bedroom.

Josef answers the door. There are several ALLIED FORCES
MILITARY POLICE in full gear. One has a gun aimed at Josef.

                    JOSEF
          Hello officers.

                    ALLIED MP 1
          Hello we are here looking for
          Josef.

                    JOSEF
          I'm Josef, I know why you are here.
          I will not resist.I just want to
          say goodbye to my wife Hanna.

The Allied offers lower their guns.

                    ALLIED MP 1
          We will give you a few moments.

                    JOSEF
          By the way Oskar is here. He is
          hiding in the bedroom.

Two of the officers walk through the living to the bedroom.

INT. JOSEF'S APARTMENT BEDROOM - DAY

The officers find Oskar in the corner shaking. They force
him up and drag him out.

INT. JOSEF'S APARTMENT - DAY

The officers are dragging Oskar.

                    OSKAR
          I can't believe you. Josef you are
          a traitor and I hate you.

Oskar starts to squirm and yell.

                    OSKAR
          Do not take me. Please. I was just
          taking orders. Josef. Help me

Josef just stands there.

                    ALLIED MP 1
          Oskar please be quiet. You are
          being arrested for war crimes.

                    OSKAR
          Josef. Please don't let them take
          me. Please...Can I go home first.

                    ALLIED MP 1
          NO. Now move...go.

The officers push and drag him out of the living room.

Josef goes over to Hanna.

                    JOSEF
          Remember what we talked about.
          Finding your family. Going to
          America. Enjoy life there.. Find a
          really nice man Have lots of Jewish
          babies... Don't forget about the
          box.

Josef Hugs her.

                    HANNA
          I remember.

Josef starts to back away then he gets close to Hanna. He
puts his hands on her cheeks. and leans in and kisses her.

                    JOSEF
          Remember live free...always.

                    ALLIED MP 1
          Josef. it's time.

                    JOSEF
          OK.

Josef walks over to them. Puts his hands behind his back.
The offers just hold his hands.

Hanna gets closer.

                    HANNA
          Officers. I want you to know, that
          Josef saved my life. He protected
          me He hated wearing the uniform..
          Josef Thank you.

Josef nods to Hanna as he is lead out the door. Hanna gets
to the door. Both Hanna and Josef start to tear up. Hanna
waves as the Officers lead him away.

Hanna closes the door and goes to sit on the couch and
starts to cry.

Hanna stops crying,and looks strait at the kitchen. She gets
up and slowly steps closer to the stove. When she gets there
she looks around. Quiet. She reaches for the box. and then
steps back and sits on the couch.

Hanna opens the box and her eyes start to water. The yellow
Jude star is on top next to her Jewish star pendent. She
reaches in and moves the yellow star out of the way and sees
the pictures.

She looks around the room. Quiet.

Hanna kisses her Star of David Pendent and holds it for a
beat and lets it fall over her heart.

She looks back to the box and sees other things in the box.
She goes through them. She goes through the pictures. and
the postcard from his brother flipping it over to see the
words. "Come to America soon, I will help you get set up
here, Family misses you. Love you brother."

She looks around the room and sees the book about America.
She flips through it.

KNOCK on the door. Hanna Jumps. She looks around for a place
to hide. KNOCK. She shakes her head.

                    HANNA
          Why am I scared?

KNOCK on door.

This time Hanna answers the door.

                    WOMAN
          Hello are you Hanna?

                    HANNA
          Yes.

                    WOMAN
          Hi, I've been trying to deliver
          this to you for a long time.

The woman Hands Hanna an envelope.

                    HANNA
          You been knocking on the door.

                    WOMAN
          Yes. I have tried several times
          over the past few years. I think
          with everything going on, you
          didn't want to answer the door.

                    HANNA
          And now.

                    WOMAN
          The war is over. I was jut told to
          hand this to you, and no other
          instructions or info. Have a good
          day.

                    HANNA
          That's it?

                              WOMAN
            Yes.

The woman leaves and Hanna closes the door.

Hanna looks at the envelope and only thing written on it is
her name.

She sits down and opens it. She pulls out a letter.

                              JOSEF (V.O)
                    Dear Hanna, if you are reading
                    this, the war is over and you are
                    now safe. I am very happy about
                    that. It also means i am a war
                    criminal. I hate the meaning of
                    this war and what it stands for. I
                    am happy I was able to protect you
                    and save your life. It is one of
                    the best things I ever did in my
                    life. I will always be proud of
                    that. Now that I am imprisoned, and
                    you are safe, I always had a dream
                    of going to America, can you follow
                    that dream for both of
                    us. Enclosed is my plan and money
                    to travel with. Please be well.
                    Love Josef.

Hanna tips the envelope and the money falls out.

INT. JOSEF'S APARTMENT BEDROOM - DAY

Hanna is packing her clothes in her suitcase. She grabs the
clothes she was wearing the day Josef found her. She takes
a deep breath and packs it.

INT. JOSEF'S APARTMENT - DAY

Hanna carries her suitcase in. She puts it down next to the
table. Opens the box and looks at the postcard.

                              HANNA
            I have a few things to do first.

Hanna opens the door takes a deep breath and steps out the
door.

EXT. ALLIED FORCES HEADQUARTERS - DAY

Hanna is heading into the building. A sign of fresh paint is
on the building.

INT. ALLIED FORCES HEADQUARTERS - DAY

Hanna walks over to an OFFICER BECKLER age about 30
American. He is helping others. Hanna waits her turn.

                    OFFICER BECKLER
          How can I help you.?

                    HANNA
          I... My name is HANNA...My husband.
          ...Josef. was brought here...he...
          He...he has been arrested.

                    OFFICER BECKLER
          For what charge?

                    HANNA
          He is a Nazi solider.

Officer Beckler looks up at her. Hanna is playing with her
Pendent. The officer notices this.

                    OFFICER BECKLER
          Um. How.

                    HANNA
          As I was trying to escape he and
          his friend Oskar caught me and my
          family, but instead of arresting
          me, he married me.

                    OFFICER BECKLER
          Oh.

                    HANNA
          Because of this. I'm still alive.
          He protect me. he never hurt me. he
          even bought me this dress.

                    OFFICER BECKLER
          So, you are here for?

                    HANNA
          Don't hurt him. I want to give him
          the same respect he gave me.

                    OFFICER BECKLER
          Ma'am, I'm not sure...

                    HANNA
          I know it's not normal.

Hanna hands over an envelope.

                    OFFICER BECKLER
          What is this?

                    HANNA
          His words and mine.on how Josef
          protected me.

Hanna starts to leave. She turns back

                    HANNA (CON"T)
          Oh. His friend Oskar other other
          hand followed the rules of the Nazi
          party. he wanted to arrest me, he
          also tried to rape me. Josef
          stopped him from that. Oskar should
          be punished.

                    OFFICER BECKLER
          Oskar, I know who you are talking
          about. He kept yelling about a
          Josef and Hanna..

                    HANNA
          I'm Hanna.

                    OFFICER BECKLER
          Hanna, We can't promise anything.
          The system well have to work. We
          will keep all this on file.

Officer Beckler takes the envelope.

                    HANNA
          Oh one last thing. . Do you know
          where I might be able to find my
          family?

                    OFFICER BECKLER
          There is a refuge camp not that far
          away...Here is the address and map
          to get there.

Officer Beckler hands Hanna a map.

                    HANNA
          Thank you officer.

                    OFFICER BECKLER
          your welcome and mazel tov on
          making it.

Hanna just looks at him. Touches her pendent.

EXT. REFUGEE CAMP - DAY

Wide shot of the camp. Hanna is walking in.

INT. REFUGEE CAMP - DAY

As Hanna walks through we see it through her eyes.

On the right side there is a board with names on it. Some
have been marked off. Hanna looks at it. She does not see
her family on it.

There are Many PEOPLE. Some are crying. Some screaming. Some
come up to her.

                    PERSON 1
               (Holding a picture)
          Have you seen this person.

                    HANNA
          Sorry, I just got here.

The person walks away. And walks to other people doing the
same thing.

                    PERSON 2
          Which camp where you.

                    HANNA
          I was lucky. I was not at a camp

                    PERSON 2
          I was at Auschwitz. Last name.
          Zucker. If you see anyone. let them
          know I'm here.

Hanna keeps walking though. She starts to cry as she sees
how the people look.

A YOUNG MAN about 20 Runs across the room almost hitting
Hanna, He yells across the room.

                    YOUNG MAN
          Papa.

                    MAN
          SON.

They hug and cry in happiness.

Hanna keeps looking around the room . She sees other
FAMILIES being reunited. and other people crying in sadness
Hanna gets to the back and she cries and can not longer
stand.

Hanna feels a tap on her shoulder. She grabs the hands and
turns and revel Rachel. They hug tight.

                    HANNA
          Rachel. I'm so happy to see you.

                    RACHEL
          Just as happy to see you sis.

                    HANNA
          I was worried about you.

                    RACHEL
          We were worried about you. After we
          heard the soldiers we had no choice
          but to leave. Papa did not really
          want too. But we had too.

                    HANNA
          I stomped my foot to signal to Papa
          to go. I wanted you guys to be
          safe.

                    RACHEL
          Papa cried, Never saw him cry
          before. Then we followed the
          tunnel. and we got to safety. We
          all did. we are all safe.

                    HANNA
          I'm so happy to hear that.

They hug again. They tear up.

                    RACHEL
          What happened to you?

                    HANNA
          I'll tell you everything, but let's
          get out of here.

                    PERSON 3
          Have you seen anyone named Zucker?

                    HANNA
          Yes. Somewhere over there on the
          left.

                    PERSON 3
          Thank you. shalom.

                    HANNA
          Shalom to you too.

There is still crying and greetings as they walk back
through.

EXT. REFUGEE CAMP - DAY

More people are arriving and leaving the camp. Hanna and
Rachel can not stop hugging.

INT. JOSEF'S APARTMENT - DAY

Hanna is getting the last of her things.

                    RACHEL
          Still can't believe this Josef
          person married you to save you.

                    HANNA
          He did. He actually turned out to
          be a nice person.

                    RACHEL
          It that him.

Rachel points to the painting on the wall.

                    HANNA
          That is him when he was a child.
          with his siblings and parents...he
          kinda looks like his dad.

                    RACHEL
          Ready to go?

                    HANNA
          Yes.

                    RACHEL
          I'll meet you downstairs.

Rachel picks up her suitcase. Hanna stops at the table. She
places an envelope at the center of the table and places the
Book of America on top. She picks up the box.

Hanna gets to the door. She slowly looks around. Takes a
deep breath. She closes the door behind her.

EXT. BOAT - DAY

A big ship is sailing on the open water.

EXT. BOAT DECK - DAY

The ship is passing Ellis Island.

                    RACHEL
          It's bigger then I thought.

                    HANNA
          Papa, Mama, You have to see this.

                    MOSHE
          Hanna. Wow. Second best thing I
          have seen this year.

Moshe gives a huge hug to Hanna.

                    GOLDIE
          We are home. Safe. Together.

The rest of the family is there too.

                    HANNA
          Home

Hanna looks down and slightly takes out the box from her
pocket.

ONE YEAR LATER

INT. HANNA'S APARTMENT - DAY

The apartment is nice. Furnished with a nice couch and a few
chairs. Next to the couch is a table. The box is on it. On
the walls is art work. Many of these are from the Old
country. A book shelve with books on it include books Hanna
brought with her.

Hanna reading as she plays with her pendent.

Rachel next to the radio is going to the beat of some music
on the radio.

                    HANNA
          Rachel, I love this song.

                    RACHEL
          You need to study.

                    HANNA
          Yes, I know. But that song is good.

                    RACHEL
          Have I told you lately that I am
          proud of you for going to school?

There is a KNOCK on the Door. Hanna does not react.

                    HANNA
          Just about every day.

                    RACHEL
          You study. I'll get the door.

                    HANNA
          Thanks Rachel

Hanna goes back to reading.

                    RACHEL
          Hanna, You have a guest.

                    HANNA
          I'm not expecting anyone.

                    RACHEL
          I think you want to talk to him.

Hanna does not take her face of out the book.

                    HANNA
          Him. Him who?

                    JOSEF
          ME!

Hanna looks up.

                    HANNA
          Um. Hi..,um...how??

                    JOSEF
          I know, Shocked to see me. I'll
          explain if you let me.

Hanna stands up and gives him a hug.

                    HANNA
          You're real. Wow. you're really
          here.

                    JOSEF
          Yes.

                    RACHEL
          I'll leave you two alone to talk.

Rachel quietly without notice backs out of the room.

                    HANNA
          Oh sorry where are my manners.
          please sit down.

Josef looks around the room and sees the table and the box.

                    JOSEF
          You have the box.

Hanna looks to the box and looks back at Josef.

                    HANNA
          Yes. I took it. I didn't want
          anything to happen to it.

                    JOSEF
          Thank you.

Hanna hands the box to Josef and he opens it.

                    HANNA
          As you were saying.

                    JOSEF
          Everything started the second i
          left the apartment and I was in the
          hall way.

FLASHBACKS

INT. APARTMENT BUILDING HALLWAY - CONTINUOUS

Josef is being escorted out by the Allied MP.

> JOSEF (V.O)
> I saw you tearing up, I was too. I
> started to tell the MP's what
> happened.

> JOSEF
> Officers. I know what I was a part
> of was wrong. I never believed in
> it. Only good thing I did was save
> her life. Her name is Hanna.

> ALLIED MP 1
> How did you do that?

> JOSEF
> The day Oskar and I found her, She
> was...

> ALLIED MP 1
> You know you will have a day in
> court and you can tell them
> everything.

> JOSEF
> OK. Just know I protected Hanna.
> Oskar wanted to hurt her.

The officers lead Josef down the hall.

INT. ALLIED FORCES HEADQUARTERS - DAY

Josef is lead in by the MP's.

> JOSEF (V.O)
> I was formally charged with my war
> crimes but as not able to tell my
> story yet.

INT. JAIL CELL - DAY

The MP's escort Josef to a cell and is pushed in.

> JOSEF (V.O)
> I was scared. at that point, i know
> exactly how you felt the day I
> found you. the not knowing.

INT. JAIL CELL - NIGHT

Josef sits quietly in the corner. On the other side of the
cell is Oskar who is angry and turns away from him.

                    JOSEF (V.O)
          It seemed like I was there forever.
          Oskar was there. He refused to talk
          to me. other people were making fun
          of him.

                    PRISONER 1
          Why are you crying baby?

                    PRISONER 2
          Cry baby Cry baby.

                    PRISONER 1
          He thought he was so macho.

                    PRISONER 2
          He's not. He asking for help

                    OSKAR
          Stop. I don't deserve this.

                    PRISONER 1
          YES you do. Just like the rest of
          us. Only thing is. I now accept my
          fate.

                    OSKAR
          Jews deserve to die.

Prisoners start to beat on him

                    JOSEF (V.O)
          For the first time I actually felt
          bad for him. Oskar always seemed to
          be in control. Now he was just
          powerless. I didn't participate
          beating him, but I didn't stop it
          either. I think for once all what
          he deserved he got. he had no more
          power over me. It was very freeing.

The MP's finally come and stop the fight. They take Oskar
out. Oskar pauses as he leaves.

                    OSKAR
          Josef, You are supposed to be my
          friend...

                    JOSEF
          You deserve that and whatever
          happens to you. All i know is I
          did the right thing for Hanna.

The MP's pull Oskar out of the cell.

INT. JAIL CELL - DAY

Josef is sitting on the bed in the cell.

                    ALLIED MP 4
          Josef, just wanted you to know that
          Oskar had his trail and he was
          sentenced. He got death. He seemed
          happy about what he did. He
          thought you were wrong. What he
          tired to do with Hanna.. sealed it.

                    JOSEF
          Thank you for telling me.

Josef just sits there.

                    JOSEF (V.O)
          I thought I would feel more about
          him being the sentence, but I was
          not. I didn't even cry. I was
          friend with him so long. But turns
          out he was not my friend. He
          controlled me. At that moment felt
          relived that he is gone.

Josef Just sits there and then looks out the window.

INT. COURT ROOM - DAY

The room is loud. Many people are talking.

                    BAILIFF
          All rise for JUDGE ZUCKER.

Everyone rises, JUDGE ZUCKER a man about 50 walks to the
bench and takes his seat.

                    JUDGE ZUCKER
          You may be seated.

                    JOSEF (V.O)
          I hardly could hear exactly what
          the judge was saying it was all
          legal stuff.

                    JUDGE ZUCKER
          Josef, how to you plea.

                    JOSEF
          Your Honor, I plea guilty of being
          on the wrong side. Following what
          my friend Oskar did.. I never
          believed in Hitler or what he
          thought. I tried not to hurt
          anyone. Only thing I can say that i
          did right was save Hanna's life. So
          whatever you do to me. I'll accept
          whatever you do to me.

The Judge rattles some papers. He picks up an envelope and
opens it. Starts to read it.

                    JUDGE ZUCKER
          I have a letter here. I am going to
          read it. To whom it may concern. I
          am writing this letter on behalf of
          Josef. I know that he says he is a
          war criminal, However all i have
          seen in him is good. I heard him
          many times complain about the war
          and hated wearing the uniform. He
          protected me for years. He could
          have turned me in, but instead
          saved me. I will always be grateful
          for saving me on so many levels.
          Please take this into consideration
          as you pass judgment on him. Thank
          you Hanna.

Josef just looks up and stares at the judge.

                    JOSEF
          Is she safe?

                    JUDGE ZUCKER
          So, your record shows that you got
          into a lot of fights.

                    JOSEF
          Yes sir, I did, they were...

                    JUDGE ZUCKER
          I see what they are about.

The judge looks at Josef.

                    JUDGE ZUCKER (CON'T)
          Josef, To my knowledge Hanna was
          reunited with her family and might
          have gone to America.

Josef just smiles.

                    JOSEF
          As long as Hanna is safe that is
          all that matters. So again whatever
          you do to me I accept.

                    JUDGE ZUCKER
          So be it.

Judge bangs his gavel

                                        FADE TO WHITE

EXT. STREET - DAY

The streets are clean and better kept. Josef is wearing
casual clothing as he strolls the street.

                    JOSEF (V.O)
          I was scared but, since I did not
          hurt anyone and how i believed and
          saving you. The letter helped...
          They let me have my freedom.

He stops at a newspaper stand. Pays for the paper DATE
reads 7. May 1946

EXT. APARTMENT BUILDING - DAY

Josef gets to the building and walks up the stairs and goes
in.

INT. BUILDING HALLWAY - DAY

Walks down the hall and goes into his apartment.

INT. JOSEF'S APARTMENT - DAY

Josef opens the door and just stands there for a moment
before entering. he looks around.

                    JOSEF (V.O)
          Coming back was strange. I was
          thinking about you as I opened the
          door. I was sad when you were not
          there. But happy that you were
          safe.

He drops the paper on the table.

                    JOSEF (V.O)
          I saw the book on the table, I
          thought about you. I thought about
          that you followed though on the
          dream of going to America. It gave
          me some pride.

Josef opens the book and sees a letter and opens it.

                    HANNA (V.O)
          Dear Josef. I want to thank you for
          all you did for me. I know by
          marrying me, you put your life in
          danger. You did not seem to care
          about that. All I know is that you
          saved me and I am and will always
          be grateful to you. I am not sure
          if you will get this letter or not.
          But if you do I want to let you
          know i followed our dream, My
          family and I went to America. You
          should still follow your dream. I
          know your family will be glad to
          see you. Be Happy and again Thank
          you. Hanna.

Josef is in tears. Looks at the book. looks around the room.

                    JOSEF
          Yes Hanna. I have a few things to
          do first.

Josef puts the letter down.

EXT. CEMETERY - DAY

Josef stands over Oskar grave.

                    JOSEF (V.O)
          I just knew what I had to do,
          Standing there I just told him how
          i felt

                    JOSEF
          Oskar you are a controlling and a
          womanizing jerk. I'm glad you are
          no longer part of my life. You have
          no effect on me and what I do
          anymore. You were wrong and you got
          what you deserved. I am now going
          to follow my dreams.

Josef stands there for a moment and then he kicks some dirt
on the grave.

INT. JOSEF'S APARTMENT BEDROOM - DAY

Josef is packing clothes and other belongs.

INT. JOSEF'S APARTMENT - DAY

Josef takes the family picture off the wall and places it in
the suitcase.

At the table Josef picks up the book of America and packs
it.

                    JOSEF (V.O)
          I packed knowing and thinking about
          my future.

Goes to the Kitchen shelve and looks around. grins.

                    JOSEF (V.O)
          I looked for the box and i could
          not find it. I realized that you
          might have taken it with you.

Josef picks up his suitcase and looks around the room.

                    JOSEF (V.O)
          For the first time in my life I was
          looking forward to something.

He turns the light off closes the door with a smile on his
face.

EXT. BOAT - DAY

A big ship is sailing on open water

EXT. BOAT DECK - DAY

Josef is alone on the deck as he sees Ellis Island.

INT. ELLIS ISLAND - DAY

Josef stands at the customs table.

                    CUSTOMS OFFICER
          From what country are you coming
          from?

                    JOSEF
          Poland.

                    CUSTOMS OFFICER
          And your name?

                    JOSEF
          Joseph. J O S E P H.

                    JOSEF (V.O)
          I thought being in America means
          having an American name.

                    CUSTOMS OFFICER
          Do you have anyone here?

                    JOSEF
          My brother Marcus.

                    CUSTOMS OFFICER
          Welcome to the United States of
          America.

The customs officer hands Josef papers Josef is smiling.

EXT MARCUS'S HOUSE.- DAY

Josef arrives and knocks on the door. MARCUS tall slender
man (38)

                    JOSEF (V.O)
          I was so happy to see my brother
          again.

They hug.

INT. MARCUS'S HOUSE - DAY

Josef looks around and sees a modern American decor style
everywhere.

                    JOSEF
          It's so good to see you.

                    MARC US
          It has been so long.

                    JOSEF
          Oskar is dead.

                    MARCUS
          Glad to hear it. He was a jerk. I'm
          just glad you are here. I called
          everyone and plan on getting
          together on Sunday...Once you get
          settled. i made up the guest room.

                    JOSEF
          Thanks.

Josef sits down. Marcus gets a postcard from the shelve.

The postcard is a picture of New York City on one side. The
other side is a note from Hanna.

                    MARCUS
          I think you need to see this.

Marcus gives the postcard to Josef. Josef reads it.

                    JOSEF (V.O)
          As I read that postcard things
          started to fit together. I know
          what happened to the box. Marcus's
          address was on a postcard. He
          helped you get settled here.

Josef smiles.

                    JOSEF
          you have her address?

                    MARCUS
          Yes. I'll get it for you.

                    JOSEF
          Wait. I have a few things i need to
          do before I see her.

                    MARCUS
          Anything I can do to help?

Josef talks to Marcus but we do not hear it.

EXT. STORE FRONT - DAY

Josef walks and stops in front of a store. A HELP WANTED
sign is in the window. Josef goes in. From the street View
Josef talks tot the OWNER of the store. They shake hands and
The owner takes the sign out of the window.

EXT. SYNAGOGUE - LATE DAY

Josef strolls on the street and walks past and stops. Makes
a few steps stops. Turns back. Looks at the building. and
then goes in.

INT. SYNAGOGUE - LATER DAY

Josef waits for the Rabbi office looking around and then the
Rabbi (older man with a full Grey beard) appears.

                    RABBI.
          How can I help you?

                    JOSEF
          I want to convert.

                    RABBI.
          Are you doing this of your own free
          will and not being forced by
          anyone?

                    JOSEF
          Rabbi. No one forces me to do
          anything anymore. I think the
          Jewish religion has lots of
          culture, meaning and history.

                    RABBI.
          Do you know anything about it
          already?

                    JOSEF
          Yes Rabbi. My wife. Taught me a
          lot.

                    RABBI.
          Your wife is Jewish?

                    JOSEF
          Yes, But she does not even know I'm
          here. She actually does not even
          know I'm in America...Long story

                    RABBI.
          I'm Listening.

                    JOSEF (V.O)
          I explained everything to him. he
          listened and understood anything.

Rabbi and Josef are talking under the Josef's speech.

End Flashback

INT. HANNA'S APARTMENT - DAY

Hanna Looks puzzled.

                    JOSEF
          I know you think i am crazy. But
          all Hitler wanted to do is kill all
          the Jewish people, but instead he
          made me become one...Though out the
          war we both thought I was saving
          you. I did protect you. What really
          happened was you saved me, You made
          me realize for the first time in my
          life I am strong enough to do what
          i want, what I feel is right, and
          follow my dreams.

Hanna smiles

                    HANNA
          You always been strong....you made
          me strong too.

Hanna picks up the box

                    JOSEF
          So glad you have this.

                    HANNA
          What is in this box makes you
          strong.

Josef opens the box and looks through the pictures and the
postcard from Marcus.

                    JOSEF
          You're right.

Josef puts the box down. Looks directly into Hanna's eyes

                    JOSEF (CON'T)
          I feel that you make me strong too.
          We seem to be connected.

                    HANNA
          We went though a lot.

                    JOSEF
          I felt strong and safe with you.
          More then with any other person.
          Almost like we belong together.

Hanna looks directly back at him.

                    HANNA
          What do you mean by belong
          together?

                    JOSEF
              (takes a deep breath)
          I ..i Love you.

                    HANNA
          What?

                    JOSEF
          I love you. I think I always have
          been.

Hanna backs away. Josef smile starts to fade.

Hanna finally walks over to Josef Looks him right in the
eyes.

                    HANNA
          I love you too.

Josef smile returns.

                    JOSEF
          I...

                    HANNA
          Not sure when it happened. I think
          When you said goodbye to me in
          Poland and kissed me. I knew. I
          been hoping ever since, you would
          find your way back to me.

                         JOSEF
               I will always find my way back to
               you. Your in my heart.

                         HANNA
               And you are in mine.

Josef pulls Hanna close and they passionately kiss.

Josef gets down on one knee.

                         JOSEF
               Even though we are already married.
               I never got to do this. So I'm
               asking will you marry me again?

                         HANNA
               YES.

They smile and hug and kiss.

INT. SYNAGOGUE - EARLY EVENING

Josef and Hanna are standing under a CHUPPA and getting
married in Jewish traditions.

INT. SYNAGOGUE - EVENING

Many People dancing the HORA. People are smiling and having
a good time.

                         RACHEL
               Mazel Tov sis.

                         HANNA
               Thanks Rachel. Mama and Paps like
               him too.

Moshe and Goldie are hugging Josef in the background.

                         RACHEL
               Strange road but you have
               happiness.

                         HANNA
               Never been happier in my life. I
               have my family, the love of my life
               and America too.

They hug. Josef, Moshe Goldie Rachel Marcus and the rest of
the family gather around. and raise their glasses.

EXT. SYNAGOGUE - EVENING

Josef and Hanna hold hands as they get into their car. They
drive off the back window has a sign JUST MARRIED

                                        FADE INTO SIGN